D0941928

Chalky

By

Dave and Pat Sargent

Illustrated by
Jane Lenoir

Ozark Publishing, Inc.
P.O. Box 228
Prairie Grove, AR 72753

Sargent, Dave, 1941-
 Chalky / by Dave and Pat Sargent ; illustrated by Jane Lenoir. — Prairie Grove, AR : Ozark Publishing, ©2001.
 ix, 36 p. : col. ill. ; 23 cm. (Saddle-up series)

 "I am forgetful"—Cover.
 SUMMARY: In 1806, a very forgetful chalky grullo horse who dreams of becoming a hero is chosen by Zebulon Pike to help in an attempt to climb the Colorado mountain later known as Pikes Peak. Includes factual information on grullo horses.
 ISBN: 1-56763-603-9 (hc)
     1-56763-604-7 (pbk)

 1. Pike, Zebulon Montgomery, 1779-1813—Juvenile fiction. [1. Pike, Zebulon Montgomery, 1779-1813—Fiction. 2. Horses—Fiction. 3. Heroes—Fiction. 4. Pikes Peak (Colo.)—Fiction. 5. Explorers—Fiction.] I. Sargent, Pat, 1936- II. Lenoir, Jane, 1950- ill. III. Title. IV. Series.

PZ10.3. S243Cha 2001
[E]—dc21   2001-000670

Printed in the United States of America

iv

Inspired by

the proud, graceful horse with the Spanish name.

Dedicated to

all kids and adults who love to watch horses graze or run through fields. And to the movie makers. What would westerns be without horses?

Foreword

Chalky Grullo is a blue-eyed silver grullo. He is a fine horse with a big problem. He is very forgetful. He has trouble remembering things.

When Mr. Zebulon Pike picks Chalky for his faithful companion, the grullo has no way of knowing that he is expected to climb the huge snow-covered mountain now known as Pike's Peak. Before they reach the summit, the sleeping camp is attacked by a vicious brown bear.

Contents

Chalky

If you would like to have the authors of the Saddle Up Series visit your school, free of charge, call 1-800-321-5671 or 1-800-960-3876.

One

The Forgetful Grullo

Dust swirled upward as the herd of horses ran around the large corral. Men were standing along the fence, watching them as they trotted passed them.

"I like the looks of that grullo," a young man said as he pointed to Chalky. "He has unusual blue eyes. That makes him a silver grullo. I need a strong horse that can travel long distances and is dependable."

"Old Chalky is certainly tough and trustworthy, Mr. Pike. I really think he would do you a good job."

Mr. Pike nodded. "I want him, and the other men in my party need good horses, too. Have them ready to go at daylight in the morning."

"Yes, sir," the foreman replied. "They'll be saddled and waiting for you."

The horses were quickly sorted into two groups. Seventeen of them, including Chalky Grullo, were taken to the barn, and thirty of them were released into the open pasture.

"I noticed our foreman did not mention your forgetfulness, Chalky," the piebald said with a big chuckle. "If he had, that Mr. Pike may have changed his mind on wanting you."

"Humph," the grullo snorted. "That man knows a good horse when he sees one. I'll make him proud of me. Just wait. You'll all see."

A moment later, he heard some-
one say, "Get out of my feed!" And
then he felt teeth nip into his neck.

The big skewbald horse pawed the air with one hoof and glared at Chalky Grullo.

"I'm sorry," Chalky said quietly as he backed away from the manger of grain. "I just forgot for a minute where I'm supposed to eat."

"You just wanted some of mine and all of yours," the irritated horse mumbled.

"No, honest," the grullo said. "It's just that I have a little trouble remembering when and where I'm supposed to be."

Chalky hurriedly backed away from the skewbald's food and looked around for his own manger. The palomino and appaloosa laughed as he quietly studied the row of stalls.

"Poor Chalky," one said. "I've never known a horse that forgetful."

"I can remember that I am going to make a very long trip with a man named Zebulon Pike tomorrow. You won't make fun of my forgetfulness anymore when I am a hero."

Laughter among the horses in the Rocking S Stables echoed within the huge barn.

"A hero?" the piebald chuckled. "You, the most forgetful horse on the Rocking S come home a hero?"

"That's right," the grullo said in a loud voice. "I'll be a hero. Then you won't laugh at me anymore."

"You're right there, Chalky," the appaloosa said with a chuckle. "You just come back home a hero, and we promise not to laugh at you anymore."

That night as all of the other horses slept, Chalky paced his stall.

"I think my friends will be proud of me when I come home," he mumbled. "I am going to prance past them with my head held high. Because I will be a . . . a . . . a . . ."

Hmmm, he thought. I can't remember what I am going to be. Only seconds later, his ears jerked forward, and he yelled, "A hero! Now I remember. Chalky Grullo is going to be a hero!"

He heard the restless movement from the other horses. Whoa there, he silently moaned. I almost woke them up.

Five minutes later, Chalky was sleeping peacefully amid dreams of a hero's welcome.

Two

Where Buffalo Roam

Three days later, the party of men were reining their horses along the banks of the Arkansas River. The silver grullo saw a large herd of strange-looking critters. Chalky's ears shot forward and he stopped. Mr. Pike laughed and explained that the animals were buffalo and that the buffalo would not bother them.

"Hmmm," the grullo muttered. "This is a strange territory. I will not forget seeing . . . seeing . . . I can't remember what he called them."

Mr. Pike reined Chalky to a halt. He shouted for his men to gather around.

"I think we better keep an eye out for renegade Indians," he told them. "They depend on the buffalo to survive."

Chalky jerked his head up.

"Buffalo! Now I remember," he exclaimed. "They're buffalo!"

The blue sky had been without any clouds since their departure from the Rocking S Horse Stables, but on the evening of the seventh day a dark, menacing cloud suddenly approached from the northwest. In ten minutes, the sun was covered, and the temperature dropped.

"A storm!" Mr. Pike yelled. "We better find some cover until it blows over."

"Good idea," Chalky muttered.

The grullo loped to the top of a hill. He stopped and looked around for a safe place to wait out the storm. He glanced toward the south and saw a long line of wagons. He pawed the ground with one hoof. But Mr. Pike was watching the storm. Chalky reared on his hind legs, his hooves pointing toward the wagons. Mr. Pike grabbed his hat with one hand and yelled, "Chalky! What's the matter with you?"

The grullo nickered and shook his head.

"Okay," Mr. Pike said quietly. "Now I see the wagon train. Come on, men. Let's join them until the storm has passed."

Chalky Grullo proudly led the party of men on horseback toward the covered wagons. The wagon master greeted them.

"Tie your horses under those trees," he yelled. "Then join us in the covered wagons. It looks like it's going to be a bad one."

The men hurriedly tied their horses under the trees. They tied them tight since it's a known fact that most horses do not like storms.

The wagon master was right. The wind blew hard, and the rain pounded against the land and everything on it as Chalky and his friends stood beneath the trees. They were not as sheltered from the storm as the people in the covered wagons, but the trees did offer them a little protection.

All the same, Chalky and the other horses held their heads low as hail pelted their backs and lightning streaked across the darkened sky.

In the early morning hours the storm stopped as suddenly as it had started. As the sun peeked over the eastern horizon, the clouds moved southward. The sun felt warm to Chalky. He yawned and stretched.

"Okay," he said. "I'm ready to start traveling again."

"Where are we going?" the skewbald snorted. "I bet you don't remember."

"I do, too!" Chalky exclaimed. "I wouldn't forget that we are on our way to . . . to . . ."

Oh, Chalky silently groaned. I don't remember where we're going. His lapse in memory was forgotten as Mr. Pike said, "I sure hope you got all rested up, Chalky, because we have a lot of exploring to do in the mountains."

Chalky looked at his friends with a smug expression on his face. "I remember. We're exploring the mountains," he declared.

It must have been about two weeks later when Mr. Pike reined Chalky to a halt. He pointed toward a massive, snow-covered peak and said, "We're going to ride to the summit of that peak!"

"Oh no," Chalky Grullo gasped. "I don't think Mr. Pike realizes how big and tall that mountain really is!"

For nearly a month, Mr. Pike's party tried to reach the top of the huge mountain. They saw lots of deer, elk, beavers, wolves, and bear. They also discovered streams and caves and studied the rocky, tree-covered terrain. One night the temperature dropped. It was extremely cold and miserable.

"I don't feel good about this," Chalky grumbled. "Winter is on the way. My common sense tells me that we should not be on top of that huge peak when it hits."

The other horses in the party murmured in agreement. Suddenly Chalky sniffed the air. Danger! He heard a noise and jerked his head toward the campfire. A huge brown bear was walking on his hind legs toward the sleeping men. His razor-sharp claws pawed the air as he approached the sleeping Mr. Pike.

For a moment, Chalky froze in fear. Then he let out a high-pitched nicker, challenging the bear to a fight to the death. The appaloosa, the palomino, the skewbald, and the piebald groaned with dread as Chalky charged toward the ferocious beast.

Mr. Pike and the other men awoke as the horse and bear collided in a fierce fight for survival.

Three

Pike's Peak

Flames from the big campfire illuminated the area as Mr. Pike and his men scrambled away from the battle between the grullo and the brown bear. Chalky's hooves lashed out at the furry beast. His teeth were bared, and his eyes were ablaze with fury. He knew that he was in a fight for his life and the life of Mr. Pike and his men.

"Get away!" he screamed to the bear. "I'll not let you hurt any of us. Just go!"

"Roar!" the brown bear replied. "I'll do what I want when I want to do it. And right now, I'm hungry!"

"I don't want to hurt you," Chalky threatened, "but I will defend Mr. Pike with my life."

Chalky's right front hoof struck the side of the bear's head, and the massive animal staggered backward.

Seconds later, the vicious critter
was lashing at the grullo's neck.

Chalky felt a burning sensation, but he lunged toward his opponent. This time, both hooves hit the bear with a tremendous force. The bear rolled onto his side and didn't move.

Suddenly a gunshot rang out through the darkness of night, and Chalky saw Mr. Pike approaching with a rifle in his hands. The bear groaned and quickly rose to his feet. A second later, he was running into the woods, away from the camp.

Throughout the night, Mr. Pike tended to the wounds on the grullo. The deep cuts from the bear claws were cleaned and bandaged before Mr. Pike sat down beside the horse. The man quietly thanked him for saving his life. Chalky lay there and soaked it up. He loved to be praised.

As daylight cast a glow upon the mountain peak, Chalky finally heard the word he wanted to hear.

"Chalky," Mr. Pike murmured, "you are my hero. I'm so proud that you are my friend."

Chalky had been on his side all night. He now felt warm and safe as Mr. Pike gently coaxed him into standing up.

The silver grullo heard words of encouragement and love from the the appaloosa, the skewbald, the piebald, the palomino, and the rest of the horses as he struggled to his feet.

Mr. Pike smiled and gently stroked Chalky's nose as he drew a deep breath and shook his body.

"I think we better postpone our trip up the peak," Mr. Pike told his men. "Winter is almost here, and we have other places I want to explore. I'm going to send Chalky home to heal and rest. We'll try this venture another time."

Whew, Chalky silently breathed a sigh of relief. It is only the year of 1806. Mr. Pike will have plenty of time to climb his peak. He smiled and mumbled, "And I could use a rest and a little heal time."

The journey down the peak was easier than the climb upward. The horses and men were a bit familiar with the paths they should take, and the trip was much faster. They again followed the Arkansas River from the tall mountain range through the foothills and onto the open plains. Chalky smiled as they passed a big herd of bison along the way.

"Buffalo," he murmured softly.

"And where did we explore, Chalky?" the piebald asked.

Chalky raised one eyebrow and winked at him before replying, "We explored rocky mountains," he said quietly. "We explored a big range of rocky mountains."

"I think that bear healed your memory, Chalky," the palomino said with a chuckle.

Three weeks later, the land was covered with the first snow of the season. Mr. Pike had sent three men and horses ahead to tell the foreman of the Rocking S Horse Stables that Chalky Grullo was on his way home. Although he was healing from his wounds, Mr. Pike was afraid that a fast trip home might hurt him. The sun was high overhead when Chalky approached the familiar big barn. Suddenly he heard loud cheers from the foreman and the ranch hands. Then he heard even louder cheers from the huge herd of horses.

"Wow! I think our friends really missed us. They're all cheering!"

"This celebration is not for us,"

the piebald said. "This celebration is for you, Chalky. You are a hero."

Then the grullo saw a sight that he would never forget. Painted above his stall the name CHALKY was written in large red letters.

"Now, Chalky, you'll remember where your stall is," the foreman said. "And a hero should have his name above his stall."

Chalky thought, I came home a hero, and folks will probably call that mountain Pike's Peak, even if Mr. Pike and his forgetful horse did not climb all the way to the summit.

Four

Grullo Horse Facts

The various groups of horse colors with black points include the grullo, a slate color. *Grullo*, which is pronounced GREW-yo, is the Spanish name for the sandhill crane, a slate-colored bird. This term is used by western riders when they refer to a blue slate-colored horse with black points and a dark or black head. Grullo horses almost always have primitive marks (withers stripe, dorsal stripe, and stripes over the knees and hocks).

33

An *olive grullo* looks like an unripe olive. And when the horse's color is smutty or dark, it is called a *smutty olive grullo.*

35

The *silver grullo* is the lightest shade of grullo. The body is a cream color, and the points and head are a slate blue instead of the black of most grullos. *Silver grullos have blue eyes*.